CW01425684

Murder is my Game

Murder is my Game

Zero Is My Name

SISTER BARBARA SUDOL
CSFN, DA

PALMETTO

P U B L I S H I N G

Charleston, SC

www.PalmettoPublishing.com

Copyright © 2024 by The Sisters of the Holy Family of
Nazareth, USA, Inc

Front Cover Photo by Edward Sudol.

All rights reserved.

No portion of this book may be reproduced, stored in a
retrieval system, or transmitted in any form by any means–
electronic, mechanical, photocopy, recording, or other–
except for brief quotations in printed reviews, without
prior permission of the author.

Paperback ISBN: 9798822976351
eBook ISBN: 9798822976368

Murder is my Game

Zero Is My Name

SISTER BARBARA SUDOL
CSFN, DA

PALMETTO

P U B L I S H I N G

Charleston, SC

www.PalmettoPublishing.com

Copyright © 2024 by The Sisters of the Holy Family of
Nazareth, USA, Inc

Front Cover Photo by Edward Sudol.

All rights reserved.

No portion of this book may be reproduced, stored in a
retrieval system, or transmitted in any form by any means–
electronic, mechanical, photocopy, recording, or other–
except for brief quotations in printed reviews, without
prior permission of the author.

Paperback ISBN: 9798822976351
eBook ISBN: 9798822976368

Dedication

For children everywhere, especially those who are not loved or nurtured, and in loving memory of George Richard Sudol.

ACKNOWLEDGEMENTS

Special thanks to Sister Kathleen Maciej, and to Sister Thea Krause and their Leadership teams for their support of this book.

Thanks to my brother. Edward Sudol, for his photograph that I used on the front cover of this book, and also his photo on the last page. You are most gracious, Ed.

My gratitude to Nicholas R. Read, Senior Publishing Consultant of Palmetto Publishing, for his time and tips during our phone conversations.

Thank you to Stephanie Kenyon for working alongside of me during the publication process.

To Megan Epperson, my grateful thanks for her creative design of the book cover.

As always, thank you to Monsignor Robert Weiss for his concern and encouragement of my efforts.

Foreword

This fictional novel is a hybrid collection of the facts and feelings of Buzz, the main character. Buzz was born into a family of grifters whose example promoted violence and upsetment into his early life, and continued the same pattern into his adulthood.

Children are not born killers. They are made so by example and circumstance. Loving adults, especially loving parents, are needed for their nurturing.

This book is fictional. Any similarity to real persons, living or dead, is coincidental and not intended by the author.

Foreword

This fictional novel is a hybrid collection of the facts and feelings of Buzz, the main character. Buzz was born into a family of grifters whose example promoted violence and upsetment into his early life, and continued the same pattern into his adulthood.

Children are not born killers. They are made so by example and circumstance. Loving adults, especially loving parents, are needed for their nurturing.

This book is fictional. Any similarity to real persons, living or dead, is coincidental and not intended by the author.

Contents

1

Playtime

Humpty Dumpty sat on a wall,
Humpty Dumpty had a great fall.

The group of youngsters twirled in an uneven circle until, one by one, they fell to the ground amid giggles as they shoved each other playfully. They got up, dusted themselves off, and proceeded to renew the same ritualistic ceremony. Ah! The innocence and creativity of children! The perseverance and resilience they reveal in play as in real life. How could one possibly know in looking at this cadre of kids that one of them might become a killer.

I stood on the sidelines looking at no one in particular. I never knew what it was to be carefree and irresponsible. From my distorted childhood I wanted everything I was denied in my childhood, but would never receive. Security, love, a family of my own? Never.

My thoughts drifted back to those kids playing. I looked at their faces, and at their clothes. They looked happy. Almost all of them seemed well cared for. I looked for the kid who was not happy. I looked for the kid who drifted off to the sidelines when he was tired of Humpty Dumpty and his falls. I looked for the kid who had hate in his eyes. I looked for me.

2

Inception

I am not going to tell you of my beginning, because I never really began in the normal sense.
Most children begin in a family setting with two
parents and maybe some siblings. They are wanted
and cared for, physically and emotionally. They are
guided until they can make decisions for themselves.
They are secure in their place in their family and
social setting. They are loved for whom they are. Yes.
But that's a lot of malarkey for someone who was
thrown into this world and landed onto a garbage
heap of twisted and soiled people and situations as
I did. So, I was incepted, if you will, not born or
raised normally. I am Zero. A nonentity.

Normality was never in my family's vocabulary.
It was Brooklyn, New York, 1920 at the beginning

3

of the Depression in America. My parents were both grifters and drifters. When one con failed, we all migrated to another run-down junk spot with our boxes and worn and torn suitcases. There we stayed, one step ahead of the Law, until we had to move again.

By now, you have the picture. My parents, Jack and Jill Black as I'll call them here were losers from the start. Those are fictitious names, of course. They are dead but probably still wanted by the Law. I could give you their descriptions, but that would only give away their identities, so I will keep them cloaked in obscurity. They never married because they never had the time or inclination to do so. They shacked up early, in their twenties, and stayed together to produce a son, and a daughter. I was their oldest whom they called Buzz. Who or what is a Buzz, I ask you? A buzz is a bee's form of communication. My parents put me early on the level of an insect.

My sister was called Helen . They gave her that name because she was beautiful from the get go, a real Helen of Troy. No surname will be given here

for Helen because she is still alive and doing well as a high-class madam. Her job takes her all over the country. You could say she is running a well-oiled machine. She is still beautiful, but ageing. Helen will know what to do when she can no longer perform adequately at her job.

I don't think my parents ever recorded our births with the Health Department. A midwife named Millie brought us into their warped world. I never saw my birth certificate or Helen's. Anonymity was our entrance into society, and continued into our childhoods. We were not schooled in the normal sense. No 9:00 to 3:00 daily schedule. It was the Depression, and many children did not attend school. Maybe they were working on their parents' farms or in their stores, or even in coal mines, or factories. We, my parents, Helen and I, were working at deceiving people. Helen and I learned how to pickpocket at the age of nine. We were clumsy at first, but got better at it as time went on. My parents set up phony businesses and went after high rollers who were the only ones who had money at that time, most of them bootleggers. As the years went on, the businesses changed as crooks became more proficient in bogus enterprises and Jack and Jill went along with the changing times.

It was tiring to be always on the run, especially when you are a little kid, but Ma and Pa made it a game. Whenever they had to do a job that was small change at first like working for the local bootlegger to deliver whiskey to local politicians who protected them, we would go along. Later, Pa got enough money to buy a used truck and Helen and I would curl up in the back seat and fall asleep, even though we were supposed to be lookouts.

Bootlegging was a remarkable swindle. Half the time, the booze was loaded with chemicals, water, and maybe a spot or two of liquor and sold and distributed as whiskey. All of bootlegging had to be done secretively because the 18th Amendment to the Constitution prohibited the sale of liquor from 1920 to its repeal in 1933. Of course, such a legal injunction led to illegal methods to obtain, sell, and distribute liquor by ingenious and sometimes dangerous approaches to circumventing the Law.

My parents were quite good at swindling. They had an innate sense of the characters with whom they dealt which only sharpened as they continued their ploys. First, they started small, learning as they went along. They worked mostly at night taking money from clients in speakeasies and driving to where the bootleggers made the whiskey which was usually in some dark hideout. There, the liquor would be poured into smaller containers maybe 10 or 20 of them, packed into the back of our truck, covered with large tarp, and sat on by Helen and me. If we were ever stopped, we quickly lay flat over the containers with a blanket over us. No cops ever checked the stuff because no one wanted to disturb two sleeping children. Pa told us it was all a game that we played with the Law, and the Law played right along with us.

The great Bank Crash of 1929 added to the creativity of my parents. Instead of shooting themselves or jumping off a tall building when they lost the little money they had, they decided to flesh out operations that were lucrative such as making their own distilled liquor, some of it from corn. The ramshack house we occupied as squatters and where Helen and I were born was perfect for making whiskey in the cellar. There were farms in Jamaica, NY that they could drive to get the corn. Unfortunately, once when they were driving through a neighboring farm, Pa couldn't slow down fast enough and killed many of the farmer's cows who were crossing the road. He found out later that the farmer lost his farm because of the loss of his registered cows. Well, such were the breaks! As long as Pa and Ma could get one step ahead of the Law, nothing bothered their consciences. They needed to live and make money. Helen and I were just two appendages who traveled along with them.

It was in 1930 that my parents were in that shack making whiskey and bringing it to a guy called Charlie. Charlie was the distributor for a politician who gave frequent parties to people as crooked as himself. We always met Charlie on Tuesday night, usually around 11:00 pm, and unloaded the booze through the basement door of his speakeasy. Even Helen and I helped to unload the containers when we got big enough. Pa told us that it was a team effort so we had to work just as much as he and Ma did.

Charlie was a short man with a red, bulbous nose. He was usually dressed in mismatched clothing with dirty work boots. His face seemed distorted because of his menacing frown. I don't think he liked any of us as he made it a point to hustle us into doing the fastest job we could of unloading the whiskey. Then he paid Pa off and quickly closed the basement door.

Actually, going into a portion of the speakeasy was a treat for Helen and me. Through a small door opening, we could see happy, well-dressed people enjoying themselves , some having animated conversations. They didn't have to worry about hustling as we did, or be concerned about their safety as we did. Even as a kid, I knew that our lifestyle was not what others lived. They were characters in a fairy tale, while we lived in a rabbit hole. Maybe it was then that I decided to get more out of my life than I was living. I began to size my parents up against the people I saw in the speakeasy, and I viewed my parents for the failures they were. Years later in conversations with Helen, she told me she hated the life our parents forced on us. but felt powerless to change it until she met Johnny who turned out to be a slick pimp.

3

Release

So, for two months, Pa made whiskey from corn and mixed it with liquor, water and methanol which proved to be a dangerous and an even deadly additive that could produce harmful effects on drinkers, even leading to death. Pa was not concerned with the safety of his clients, only with the money they produced.

As usual, we took the liquor down to Charlie around 11:00 pm on a Tuesday night. But we were in for a big surprise. For two months Pa had been making and selling dangerous concoctions to the speakeasy. When we arrived, two other men were waiting outside for the delivery. They were big and they wasted no time grabbing Pa by his throat and accusing him of paralyzing Charlie and a number of "guests" in the speakeasy by the liquor he sold.

"You half assed jack nape. Now you're going to pay," they grunted as they took turns chocking, punching, and kicking Pa until blood spouted out of his mouth and dark bruises began to appear on his face. He groaned and kept rolling over holding himself in pain while attempting to get away from the two brutes. When the two men finished beating Pa, they went to the truck, opened every container of the distilled liquor and poured it over Pa's face and body.

Ma, Helen and I stood rooted. None of us tried to intervene because we were afraid they would go after us next. After they poured the whiskey on Pa, they threw the containers on the ground, straightened up, and glared at the three of us.

"Don't come here again if you know what's good for you," they grunted. "Get this jack ass out of here before we kill him." With that warning, they went into the speakeasy and shut the door.

Pa lay writhing in pain on the ground. We all went up to him, and tried to get him as easily as possible off the ground and into the truck. I will never forget how badly deformed he looked, how he cried aloud with each movement, dripping with excessive amounts of blood, and, in the end, mercifully, he blacked out so that we could lay him down in the back of the truck, and cover him with the blanket. Ma never got a driver's license, but she knew how to drive. She started the engine and quickly eased the truck out of the driveway and into the main road. She drove to the Millie's house, woke her up with pounding on her door, and got her to come to the truck and take a look at Pa.

Pa looked like he was dead, except we could hear the labored breathing that emitted from his chest. When Millie examined him, he opened his eyes in a frantic stare as if he felt he was going to be beaten again.

"You have to get him to a hospital" Millie told Ma. "He is losing a great deal of blood, and his breathing sounds as if some of his ribs are broken."

"We can't do that, Millie. You know that. Just help us as much as you can. Can you keep him in your house in a bed? I'll stay with him and do whatever you tell me to do." 'Please, Millie!" Ma frantically asked.

"Ok", Millie agreed, but spotting Helen and me, she asked, "What about the kids? I have no room for them."

Ma thought for a long moment, then turned to me and told me to take Helen and to get into the truck, "When we get Pa into Millie's house, I'm going to drive you and Helen home. There I want you to stay until I come and get you. Understand?"

I was 13 at the time and Helen was 12. We helped get Pa into a bed in Millie's house, and Ma drove us home, to the dump we squatted in. There we stayed for two weeks while Pa recuperated with Ma and Millie at his side. Besides being the local midwife, Millie was a nurse who worked shifts in a local hospital. She knew a lot, and what she didn't know she asked a certain doctor who was sweet on her. He was the one who came to see Pa and to evaluate his condition. Pa had three broken ribs, a badly discolored face with a smashed in nose, a dislocated shoulder, and a bruised kidney that would give him trouble for the rest of his life due to the pulmonary edema it often produced. The doctor gave Millie morphine to block Pa's pain before he wrapped Pa's ribs and he jerked Pa's shoulder back into its socket. He gave Millie bandages and ointments to cover Pa's open wounds that were beginning to fester, Pa's nose would heal into the misshapen way the thugs broke it.

In the meantime, Helen and I stayed in the shack and ate what we could steal. We tried to keep clean and look presentable so that no one would suspect that we were living without parental supervision. Ma came once a day to check on us and to give us details about Pa's condition. It was a horrible time to live through. Of course, Pa needed all of Ma's attention as he recuperated, but where did that leave us? We were still kids who also needed her.

Slowly, the realization dawned on me that I was not a child anymore, and, like it or not, I needed to begin fending for myself. I needed to get out and fast. I felt sorry for Helen, but I couldn't take her with me. She was still a child both physically and emotionally. It was better for her to stay with our parents.

The thoughts of my release began to overwhelm me. I had already determined for myself that my parents were has-beens struggling to keep intact in a losing game, I did not imagine myself missing them, as I had realized long ago that the only reason, they kept us was because they had brought us into their mixed-up world and would keep us only until we got too much in their way. I felt badly for thinking this way, but the squalid reality of our lives together had become clearer each day.

So, where could I go and be able to live on my own? Pa needed to stay at Millie's house for another two weeks. He was really broken, not only physically, but mentally. His source of income was gone, Ma was exhausted from nursing him, Millie wanted him and Ma out of her house, and, least of his worries, Helen and I were existing without much food, proper shelter, and with the insecurity of an uncertain future.

I had no friends or teachers to advise me. I only knew Ma, Pa, and Helen. Wherever I was going to end up would be my decision. I thought back to the speakeasy. Maybe they would hire me for errand jobs. I was tall for 13 and my voice had begun to change. Maybe I could pass for 16 or 17. I had to try.

It was 6:00 am and Helen was asleep when I slipped out of the dump we called home. I felt bad not to say goodbye, but I knew she would kick up a fuss and make it harder to leave. I packed a suitcase with a few clothes and a picture of the four of us, and walked the 10 miles back to the speakeasy, avoiding main roads so no cop on patrol would pick me up.

4

An Education

When I got to the speakeasy which was called, ironically, The Rose, I paused, took a deep breath, and knocked timidly on the front door. The door was opened by a genial looking man whose name I later found out was Mike.

"Well, what do we have here? What can I do for you?"

"I'm looking for work," I stammered in a husky voice.

"And what kind of work can you do?" Mike asked.

"Tell me what you need and I'll do it," I answered, trying to impress Mike with my know-it-all attitude

Mike peered at me as if he was trying to uncover my true motivation. Was I a felon, an undercover decoy sent by the cops, or just a tired, hungry kid who needed a job?

"Come in," Mike said. Are you hungry?"

"Yes. A little," I replied.

"Sit over there by the table and I will get you some food."

I sank into a soft chair by a wide table. The faint smell of cigarettes lingered in the room. I looked around. The room was a sort of kitchen and waiting area with brown cabinets holding dishes, glasses, and silverware. There were two cavernous sinks, an icebox, stove, and shelves. Four round tables with soft, upholstered chairs completed the scene.

People began to drift in and to sit at the tables. They looked at me curiously as I stared back at them, but no one questioned my presence and I was afraid to say anything that would jeopardize my hope of getting a job. Mike, apparently, was the chef who was making breakfast for the group clustered around the tables. The smells of eggs, bacon, fritters, fresh bread and coffee almost overwhelmed me. I hadn't had a good meal in weeks, and I looked forward to devouring such a meal.

Mike must have understood that I was famished and served me first piling my plate with as much food as it could hold. Then he poured a generous amount of coffee into a large mug, and stood back for a moment looking intently at me as I started to devour this delicious meal. Realizing he had other people to serve, he turned and began filling large platters of food on the tables and setting huge coffee pots on each table as well.

I concentrated on the great meal, but every now and then I looked around me at the people sitting at the tables. No one was talking loudly. After a short while, they finished their food, thanked Mike, got up, and left the room. I found out later that they were the waiters, bus boys, and waitresses for the speakeasy. Only now it wasn't called a speakeasy but a salon or a fancy restaurant that opened at night and served a very select clientele. Even later, I discovered that The Rose was a cover for a very profitable prostitution business controlled by the infamous crook Steve A., a hood from the streets of Brooklyn who had made a name for himself in crime.

Mike was watching me carefully as I watched the people leaving the tables. Finally, he asked me if I had enough food? I was full, and smiled as I thanked him, and asked again for a job.

"Where are your parents, kid?" Mike wanted to know.

"I ran away from them. They don't want me and I don't want them," I answered truthfully.

"How old are you?"

"I'm 16" I said, hoping he would believe the lie I told.

"Kid, you are no 16, or I'm a monkey's uncle!" Mike retorted. "If you are all of 13, that's all you are. Never con a con man., kid, especially me if you want a job here," Mike said impatiently.

My red face told him that he was correct. I looked at him, but said nothing, expecting to be thrown out without further ado. Mike thought a moment and then told me they needed a janitor, someone who could clean up after the staff had finished their meals in the kitchen, and the patrons had left the restaurant.

"You will call me Mr. Mike. You'll get three meals a day, a cot in the back room, and $5.00 a week if you want the job, with one day off a week. You will work as many hours as we need you, and you will keep your eyes open and your mouth shut if you know what's good for you. You will report directly to me, and if I ever see you slacking, or telling anyone about what goes on here, I will haul your sorry ass out of here in a basket. Got all that, kid?"

Too shocked to say anything but yes, I nodded affirmatively.

"O.K. So, what's your name?"

I told him my name was Buzz. I felt there was no need to tell him my last name, as I wanted to sever myself completely from my parents. Mike didn't question me further, but took me to a back room that had a cot, a closet for clothing. and a washbasin. He showed me the toilet in the hallway, and the janitor's closet that contained brooms, mops, pails, and dusters.

"Did you bring anything with you—clothes, shoes, a toothbrush?" Mike asked.

Yes, I have a few things I said. not wanting to explain my sudden departure from my family.

Mike grunted to himself and told me to follow him to a room upstairs where he fitted me with overalls, shirts, shoes, and gave me some fancy toiletries.

Mike then took me downstairs and showed me the restaurant which, to me, was a gilded palace.

"This place opens at 5:00 pm and closes at 1:00 am, every night. It will be your job to keep it clean, and to put supplies in the rooms and bathrooms."

Mike then took me to the five rooms in the back, each one containing a soft, wide bed, a liquor cabinet, and a dresser with a large mirror.

"This is where our girls work at night. The head of this operation is Twana. She will tell you which rooms to clean, and what supplies are needed. She takes care of the bedding. You only are around these rooms to clean them during the day. Get it?'

I nodded affirmatively. Turning a corner, Mike walked over to a large room with green double doors. He opened the doors, and switched on the light.

The room was large enough to seat at least 50 people at a time, maybe more. There were tables for blackjack, roulette, poler, and faro. Surrounding the tables were bell slot machines. In the back of the room were tables set up for food that was prepared in a kitchen with large windows. Against the wall was an array of all types of liquor, a space for at least three bartenders, and a large circular seating area. At the backs of either end of the seating area were two doors with the words Private printed in large letters.

The walls were ornamented in gold against a light rose paint. There were large pictures of nature as well as of half-dressed women. In the center was a large chandelier, and throughout the room hanging from the ceiling were several smaller chandeliers.

Mike watched me as I took the room in. I was overwhelmed by the opulence and the sheer luxury that was there. It was a true mecca for gamblers. Every piece of furniture, every item had been placed to give effect. The soft rose-colored walls with gilded trimmings gave off an ambiance that encouraged intimacy and familiarity. Even the hanging smell of cigarette and cigar smoke told of a haven for a special group of people who knew each other and the purpose for which they came. And, the best of it all was that they were protected. They were secure from interference by the Law because of Steve A, who .paid off the local politicians not to interfere. It was the best con job I had ever come across, and I began to feel grateful that I might become a part of it.

Mike couldn't resist chuckling as he viewed my astonishment .

"Never seen a place like this before, have you, kid?"

"No sir," I answered, too overcome to say anything.

"Well, you'll be seeing a lot more of it because you will be cleaning it with another kid whose name is Carl. I will introduce you to him tomorrow. Now, take the rest of the day to get your stuff together, and to get to know the place. Stay out of the rooms that are marked Private. You are never to go into them. Get it?"

I said yes, and Mike led me out of the gambling room, shut the lights, and closed the doors. Then he took me to the back room with the cot that was to be my bedroom, told me that he would have a dresser brought up for my use, and asked if I needed anything else? I said no, and he left to prepare lunch for the workers.

I sat down on the cot, too overwhelmed even to think. For the first time in my life, there were going to be three meals a day to eat, more than one set of clothes and shoes to wear, a toilet of my own to use, four strong walls surrounding me, and the assurance of guidance from an adult. I laid back on the cot which was really a small bed, and promptly fell asleep.

5

In the Meantime

Ma came home about 8:00 pm to check on Helen and me. She did this routine every night, dragging herself away from caring for Pa and from putting up with Millie's constant badgering question of when the hell she and Pa was going to get out of her house? Millie was afraid that the neighbors would notice Ma's goings and comings from Millie's house, or, worse still, that the men who had beaten Pa up would look for him to kill him if any more people from the speakeasy had been paralyzed, or died from the tainted liquor he sold them.

When Ma came back to the shack the day I left, she asked Helen where I was. Helen tearfully replied that she didn't know, that I had been gone from early morning, and had not told her where I was going. Ma was too tired to think, and did not have too much time to worry about my whereabouts as she had to get back to nursing Pa. She asked Helen if she had enough food to eat. Helen said she hadn't eaten all day, so Ma gave her two dollars to buy something for herself. Of course, it was already night. Where was Helen supposed to shop for food? All the stores were closed.

That fact did not enter into Ma's mind. She sat wearily down on the torn easy chair in what was designated as our parlor. She put her feet up on a box, and promptly fell asleep, exhausted between taking care of Pa and Millie's harping.

Helen looked at Ma, and went into her bedroom. She was hungry, tired, and worried about me. She wondered why I had left without saying goodbye. More importantly, why hadn't I taken her with me? She mulled over the fact that I might be gone for good, and felt a heavy sadness come over her. We had been inseparable. I had always looked out for her, and had even protected her from the rotten life we lived with our swindling parents. I had made sure she had enough to eat, even if it meant I had less. I made sure she was warm enough at night by plugging up the drafty cracks in the dump we lived in. Most of all, I was always there by her side since we were babies. If I had left for good, Helen thought, she was agonizingly alone. That feeling of deprivation was too much to bear. Helen threw herself on her bed and wept bitter tears.

Ma woke up to Helen's convulsive crying and she sensed that I was gone and for good. Ma understood that Helen had always depended on me rather than on herself and Pa. Well, Ma thought, Buzz had had to leave sometime, so this was no great surprise to her. Ma only wished that I would make out okay in the crazy world she, Pa, and Helen lived in.

Thinking of Helen, Ma wondered what their life would be like for Helen, now that I was gone. She was only 12 and could not survive by herself. It really wasn't safe for Helen to be alone all day in this shanty, and Millie would never tolerate taking Helen in. Ma knew that Pa would have to be moved back here. She knew what to do for Pa as long as Millie continued to supply the drugs Pa needed to recover. Moving Pa needed to be done at night, Ma thought, probably this night, so no curious onlookers would know who had been in Millie's house.

Ma got up from the chair and went to Helen's room. She quietly opened the door and looked in. Helen was awake, her face drenched with tears. She looked at her mother, and waited.

"Helen, tonight I am bringing Pa home. You won't be alone. Buzz has probably gone out on his own, but the three of us are still together. Come with me to Millie's house to get Pa."

At that, Ma left the room. Helen got up from her bed, put her coat on, and followed Ma to the truck to get Pa. There was no conversation between them. They both knew that life was tough and only the tough would survive the life they were living.

6

Going Deeper

The next day for me brought a new series of surprises for me. Mike showed me what places needed to be cleaned and I met Carl, an 18-year-old, six-foot, ugly dispositioned, goof who in my estimation wouldn't amount to much in this world. He was gangly and his movements were those of a walking giraffe. His head moved first and the rest of his body followed behind. It wasn't enough that he looked stupid, but that he was stupid. That's the only way I could describe him. He had been at the job for two months, cleaning the various rooms, but he never could figure out what he had to do. Mike was very patient with him, explaining the same directions every day and almost pushing him where he had to clean next. Carl probably realized that he was not the brightest diamond in the deck and that knowledge frustrated and angered him. Right from the get go, I think he realized that I would outshine him, and, possibly, that Mike had brought me on because he was tired of telling Carl what had to be done day after day. So, Carl hated me from the beginning. He never spoke to me except to pass rude comments to me and about me.

But, I didn't care about Carl as long as I pleased Mike. Mike slowly became the only real father I had ever known. He watched over me, corrected me when I needed it, and saw that I had enough to eat and good clothes to wear. He did not allow me to mingle much with the other adolescents and young people who worked in the establishment. At night, for an hour or so, after the kitchen was cleaned, he sat me down at one of the tables and began teaching me to read and to write. By then, Carl was gone and I had Mike's complete attention.

The years passed quickly. I moved from janitor to busboy to waiter to Mike's personal assistant. I now had a private bedroom with all the accommodations some of the wealthier patrons of the business had. Mike had bad arthritis in his spine and progressively needed to sit and stretch out his legs, so I became his personal secretary and errand boy. Mike trusted me to the degree that one day, he took me into an office that had the word Private on it, a place that had been off limits to me since I arrived six years ago, as a 13-year-old, scared hungry kid.

In the six years I was with Mike, I saw Ma, Pa, and Helen every month . Mike allowed me to visit them in the apartment they now lived in and to bring them a generous amount of cash to help them out. Pa couldn't work, or, rather, was so traumatized by the beating he had been given that he refused to do anything that might bring some income in. He never stepped a foot outside the apartment. Ma badgered him daily and he responded by putting on a sick act every time. Ma worked at the hospital cleaning after patients. Millie had found her that job.

Helen was a beauty at 18, and caught in the web of their plight. She found work as a seamstress in a factory, a dead-end job that slowly ate away at any sense of pride in her knowing she could do better if given half a chance. She clung to me during my visits and begged me to take me with her, but, of course, I couldn't. The only job opened to young girls in The Rose was that of a prostitute. I would never allow her to do that. Yet, I knew that she was becoming more desperate and would jump at the first chance to get out of the hell hole she was in. But, for the time being, both Ma's and Helen's incomes, plus the money Mike generously provided allowed all three of them to live in the first real home they ever had.

Both my parents never questioned my leaving them as early as I did, nor did they raise concerns about the work I was doing. Their general questions only received general answers from me. They were too occupied in keeping afloat in their own lives and situations to worry about me—not that they had ever seriously been anxious about my welfare.

So our lives went on. Drudgery for Helen, monotony for Ma and Pa, and status for me. It wasn't long before I became part of the establishment that governed The Rose.

7

In the Hood

The first time Mike took me into the room marked Private, I was 19 years old. Mike had groomed me for this encounter of my life because I met Steve A., , hood, par excellence, who worked with his boys in Brooklyn and in the lower East Side of New York.

Steve was surrounded by at least six very serious looking guys. If Mike hadn't brought me in, I think they would have roughly frisked me, and then thrown me aside. Steve was smiling, his customary response, as he grabbed my hand and shook it firmly.

"So, you are Buzz. Mike told me you are his assistant, so he must trust you," he said as he scrutinized me from top to bottom.

"Yes, sir," I stammered unable to talk because my mouth had suddenly gone dry in fear.

"Well. Well. Did Mike tell you why you are here?"

"No, sir," I said while choking on my words. All of a sudden, I felt terrified as to what Steve was going to ask me to do.

He told me to sit down and listen. I sat next to Mike, as if to have his protection.

Steve got right down to business. All the men in the room sat at the large rectangular table with him at the top. The men had already been served drinks, and now turned their attention to their boss. He pointed to a large map on the wall.

"Tonight, around midnight in Atlantic City, there will be many crates delivered on the dock. Those crates will be loaded on to two trucks and brought to New York City where they will be unloaded at the Ravenite Social Club, 247 Mulberry Street in Little Italy," Steve said as he pointed on the map to that area.

"The crates contain heroin which is worth a fortune. Colin T. will be at the Club waiting for this shipment. Turning away from the map, he looked at all of us intently.

"Only, the shipment will never arrive at the Club. One of the men in each truck will be you, Rocco, and you, Mickey. You will force the drivers to cooperate, or else get rid of them. Then, both trucks will be driven to Augustino's Restaurant in Hoboken, New Jersey. There, the rest of us will reload the shipments as quickly as possible. We don't have too much time. Colin T. and his men expect the trucks to come in to New York around 3:00 am. We need to get them to Hoboken by 2:00 am, reload them into our own trucks by 2:30 am, and bring the entire stockpile to my home on Staten Island. We will leave the heroin there in my secure hiding place until T. cools down, even if it takes months. Even if he wants to search this place, he will never find the heroin, so he won't suspect us. Got all this, so far?," Steve asked, looking specifically at me.

"Yes, sir," I gulped. I wanted to run out of that room as fast as I could, realizing the enormity of the crime I was to be involved in. But Mike was the comforting presence at my side even though he said nothing.

"Okay, Buzz. Here's your part in all this business. You and Mike will be in the back of one of our trucks. When we get to Atlantic City and the heroin is unloaded, you two will be lookouts for the cops or anyone else who interferes. The same applies when we unload in Hoboken. Mike will give you a gun and show you have to use it. He already has his. Got that, Buzz?"

I sat embedded in my chair. I knew this job was going to be the biggest test of my young life, and if I screwed it up, I was toast. Mike nudged me to say something.

Boosting up my confidence, I replied that I was willing to take this job and to do well in it.

Steve looked carefully at me, and then at Mike.

"This kid has a lot of spunk, Mike. Keep him close. If he does well, there will be many other jobs we can use him for."

With that remark, Steve turned back to the other men at the table and Mike motioned me to leave the room with him.

Mike asked me how I was feeling as we walked slowly back to the kitchen. I could tell his spine was giving him arthritic pain and he needed to sit down again and rest.

"I'm okay, Mike. I just need to do some thinking," I said.

"Don't overthink this job, or you will get too scared to do it. The first time is always the hardest. After that, it gets easier," Mike said.

I asked Mike if such jobs ever really got easy. He just smiled and began to give directions to the chef who had replaced him, because he was now debilitated by his constant pain.

8

The Heist

Mike and I were in the truck, driving to Atlantic City to pick up the heroin. We were in the back sitting on the side benches and holding on for dear life. The driver wanted to be at the dock earlier than midnight, so he hit the gas pedal to the floor and lunged the truck forward. The road was mostly empty of other traffic so his speed did not cause any problems to other drivers. Mike was in a reflective mood. I asked him what he was thinking. He looked at me with that kind smile of his and told me that this was his last job for Steve.

"You know, Buzz. I've been doing this work since I was a little older than you are now. My parents were very poor in Ireland, and there were six of us children in our family. My father was a farmer and my mother took in laundry. Each of us was expected to do his share on the farm and in the house. Well, I got tired of farming. For me, it was monotonous work—drudgery, day after day, week after week, year after year. I got tired of the smell of dirt and horse manure."

"One day, Tim, a friend of mine from school, told me that he was running away to Dublin where he hoped to get on a boat and sail to America. He asked if I wanted to join him. Well, he didn't need to ask twice. I really didn't think thar I might never see my parents or brothers and sisters ever again. I just knew I had to get out of the monotonous life I was leading. So, that's what I did. Tim and I planned to leave on Monday of next week. I carefully got together what I thought was necessary, scraped together some money that I was saving, and got ready to leave my parents and siblings behind."

"The boat trip was long and monotonous. We bunked in steerage where there was little air, and no privacy. Many immigrants from other countries had the same idea as we did. Go to America, the land of the free, and make a fortune. Not many of them realized that dream, at least not immediately."

"But, when we saw Lady Liberty as the boat neared Ellis Island, we felt like we were kings, ready to rule the world."

"Reality struck home soon enough. Tim had an uncle who met him after he passed the Immigration Center. Tim asked his uncle if he could take both of us to his home, but his uncle had a large family and barely had room for Tim. Well, off they went, and I stood at the corner of the Center, not knowing what I would do next or where I could go.

"I decided to get out of the immigration Center, and I walked along the dock. Other boats and ships were anchoring. People of every class were walking with luggage, meeting family members, or just getting in the lines to be inspected and passed through Customs".

"It was already midday and I was hot, tired, and hungry. There was a park nearby with lots of shady trees. I walked there and sat under a big oak and promptly fell asleep".

Mike stopped for a long moment. I could tell the pain in his spine was beginning to irritate him, probably because of his sitting in the same position for so long. We were getting closer to Atlantic City.

I sensed that Mike wanted to tell his story before we got there, so I waited for him to finish.

" From bring in that park to being here for this heist, I wandered picking up whatever work I could get. I did pretty much what you did, Buzz. I looked for work in the speakeasy, and fell in with the Steve's gang. They taught me how to steal, fight, do drugs, embezzle, and even kill. I'm not proud of what I've done. My life was empty until you came looking for work as a young kid. I began to realize then that I would never have a home of my own, or a wife or children. Maybe that's why I took you under my wing.. And that's why this will be my last job. I've talked it over with Steve. He says I can retire to Florida if I want to, and I can take you with me—that's if you want to go with me."

You could have thrown me for a loop. Here I was on the brink of proving myself as a gang member, and Mike was ready to cut out. Mike must have seen the confusion on my face. I didn't have time to answer as the truck was slowing down and then came to a complete stop.

We waited quietly, then Mike got out of the truck and looked around. The other truck came along side and all of us got out. We waited for the boat to dock, and our men went into the boat to begin unpacking the crates with the help of steel girders wrapped around each crate. Mike and I both had our guns out, cautiously looking over the entire scene. It was close to midnight and very dark. There was no other movement but ours and that of the men unloading the heroin. Mike and I walked the length of the dock back and forth until the men signaled that all the crates were in the trucks. The men driving the trucks for Colin T. were instantly shot in their heads by Rocco and Mickey who then shoved their bodies into the Atlantic City Waterway, and got into the trucks to drive.

We arrived as planned in Hoboken. The heroin crates were unloaded and then reloaded into other trucks belonging to Steve to be driven to his home on Staten Island. Steve himself was on hand to thank his men, and paid them off. Then they got into a waiting car and sped off to live undercover until the heat from this job both from the cops and from T's gang would die down.

Steve thanked me personally, gave me $200. for my work, and sent me home in another car with one of his men. I wondered why Mike wasn't coming in the car with me, but it was almost 5:00 am and I was very tired from the stress of the entire affair. I got into the car and fell promptly asleep.

Steve asked Mike to come to Staten Island with him. It was considered an honor to drive in the same car with him, one that Mike had never experienced before. Steve didn't speak much during the drive, except to thank Mike, comment on my worth for future operations, and ask whether Mike still wanted to retire. Mike answered affirmatively, and reminded Steve that he had asked to take me to Florida with him. Steve nodded his head and fell silent again.

They arrived on Staten Island around 6:30 am. It was a clear day. The sun was brightening the shadowed building as the car passed the gate where two men guarded the entrance to Steve's mansion. The gate closed behind the car which drove up a long driveway stopping before the front steps of the entrance. Mike had never been to the boss's mansion. It was a magnificent structure in every sense of the word. Red and white brick, arched tall windows, a second-floor balcony that extended the length and width of the house, and a manicured garden was what Mike took in before he followed the boss into the house and into an adjoining sitting room.

"Make yourself at home, Mike" Steve said affably as he went to a liquor cabinet and poured whiskey into two glasses, giving a glass to Mike.

"Thanks, Boss. You certainly have a beautiful home."

"Yes. It's the best that money can buy. Just relax here for a bit while I go to get the crates unpacked and loaded into my safe. I am sure by now that Colin T. knows he's been tricked and is frantic to know who robbed him."

With that, Steve left the room with his glass in his hand. Mike slowly drank the whiskey and took in the room's furnishings. The highlight of the room was a magnificent, large oil painting of the boss himself, sitting on a red velvet chair like a king overlooking his kingdom. Mike thought that the Steve should have been holding a scepter, but then he remembered that Steve's scepter was a gun.

Mike adjusted himself in the seat, took a long drink of the whiskey, and closed his eyes. I am sure he thought of me and wondered if I would come with him to Florida. Yes, Florida. Nice warm sunshine. and less pain in his hips. No more heists, and no more killings He began to feel very drowsy, and did not hear the small opening in the painting that allowed a sawed-off Zombie Kill shotgun to shoot directly at him. All he felt was a sharp pressure that exploded first his face, and then his entire head, Then he felt nothing. Slumping over in the armchair, bones and blood pouring from his open skull, Mike was no more.

Steve entered the room minutes later with two men who had rags and a canvas body bag. The men went right to work putting Mike in the bag and cleaning the area, getting rid of the armchair which was soaked with blood, and replacing it with a new one.

Steve looked at Mike's obliterated head before he was placed in the bag, and said, half to himself, that no one retires from the gang.

9

Maturity At a Price

I learned of Mike's death through Joey, a former bus boy turned hood whom I knew while I was growing up in the speakeasy under Mike's care. For a week, I had expected to see Mike at the restaurant after the heist but he never showed. I was afraid to ask questions but my fear that something had happened to him kept growing along with my painful sense of loss. Then, one day, Steve came up to me and told me in a very sorrowful tone of voice that Mike had had a massive heart attack while at his house last week, and they had to bury him quietly because of his known dealings to the cops. He had been cremated, placed in an urn, and buried in a secret spot on Staten Island.

"We know how close you and Mike were, but for your safety, we can't let you know anything further," Steve told me. "Leave it at that. Just remember how good Mike was to you."

With that cryptic message,—and veiled warning—to me, Steve turned and walked away. Except that I didn't believe a word he said to me. Mike did not have heart trouble. He had arthritic spinal pain, but that was it.

I began to feel two very strong conflicting emotions: a deep sense of loss for Mike, and a growing desire to kill the boss whom I felt was responsible for Mike's death. I was determined to find out how Mike really died. Getting even with Steve might take years, but however long it took, he would pay with his life for taking the life of the only father and friend I ever truly had.

So I snooped around quietly, trying to find out the circumstances of Mike's death. One day as I was driving with Joey to shake down a bar tender to whom we gave protection, and who had not come across with the money he owed the boss, I flat out asked Joey if he had heard anything about Mike's death. It was a dangerous move to make, but Joey and I had been paired for several months doing small jobs like collecting bribes, beating up those who wouldn't cooperate with Steve's demands, and even kneecapping anyone trying to escape our orders. I felt that Joey wouldn't rat me out, so I took the chance. Joey was quiet for a while. I began to get nervous. Then he told me that Mike had been shot by Steve's hoods in his Staten Island home on the morning after the big heist of heroin. His men took Mike's body in a bag to the tip of Staten Island, rented a small boat and took it out to the deepest part of Narrows Bay, weighed the body bag down with huge stones and tossed it overboard. Joey said that one of the men yelled out "Sleep with the fishes, Mike" as they hauled Mike into the Bay.

Nothing can describe the combined anger and anguish I felt at hearing how Mike died without a friend, and at the hands of thugs following the orders of the boss. I was grief stricken that I could not have prevented such a heinous act on someone who had been the only person, with the exception of my sister Helen, who cared for me and had guided me. And to die this way?! I started to howl with grief and anger. Joey drove the car to a wooded area so no one would hear my screams. I jumped out and ran and ran through the brush until I flung myself on the ground and beat the dirt with my fists while my entire body heaved with sobs.

After I quieted down from exhaustion, I sat up and stayed motionless for about 10 minutes. And then the bitterness that was to be with me for the rest of my life began to form. I would never let anyone or anything hurt me again. It was also then that I conceived the desire to wreak vengeance on Steve and, ultimately, to do far worse to him than he had done to Mike. I would bide my time, and he would never suspect what I was going to do.

I had another problem to worry about. Helen had met a guy, Johnny, who fascinated her, She told me that she was falling in love with him and that she wanted to marry him. Helen was 19 at the time. What did she know of love? Our family certainly didn't prepare her for love and marriage. I had to find someone to talk to her, woman to woman, so that she would at least have an idea of what she was getting into. And, I needed to find out more about this guy, Johnny.

I set up a meeting with Helen and Twana, our

local madam. I prepared Twana to look like and act like a motherly woman who was experienced in matters of the heart. Well, Twana was certainly experienced as she had directed the prostitution business in The Rose for a number of years. However, she understood my concern for Helen and agreed to meet her.

The next person to meet on my agenda was Johnny. I set up a day and a time with Johnny and went to meet him in Little Italy on a Saturday morning.

10

Helen

Helen didn't know I was meeting with Johnny. She agreed to meet with Twana who told me after their meeting that Twana had persuaded Helen to wait and not to marry the first guy who came down the pike. I was relieved, and now I had to convince Johnny to lay off Helen and find some other dame to bother.

I met Johnny in the local saloon. He was 26 at the time, and from what I found out, a real ladies man. He had no criminal record, but I didn't like him from the start. He was too flashy, too much in my face. While he was talking to me, he was sizing up the women at the bar. I started to talk to him about his relationship with Helen, and he told me not to worry. He knew that Helen was in love with him, but he was not the marrying kind. I told him he had the right attitude as far as not marrying Helen was concerned. I told him the best thing he could do would be to stop seeing her altogether. Tell her anything, but break up with her. He looked me straight in the eye and told me not to worry. He would take care of everything that night when he and Helen got together.

I shook hands with him, but I knew I couldn't trust him as far as I could throw him. And, I wanted to throw him right through the bar window. Instead, I turned and left. There was a gnawing doubt in me about Johnny. I felt he was up to no good concerning Helen. So, I decided I would visit her the next day and see for myself how sincere he really was about breaking up with her.

I went to my parents' apartment on the following afternoon. Ma opened the door. She had been crying and looked at me wearily.

"If you're looking for Helen, she's not here. She ran off with that good for nothing Johnny. He sweet talked her into eloping with him. She wouldn't tell me where she was going, but she told me to tell you not to try to find her. She said she has to live her own life just as you left to make your own life."

I was furious. I went to my father and demanded to know why he had allowed Helen to leave with Johnny. But he was useless. He was in his own little world, far, far away. He had never gotten over his beating, and his years of isolation from any connection with the outside world had progressively cut him off from reality. He just stared at me, not comprehending why I was so angry.

I turned back to Ma. I clumsily put my arm around her, not even knowing how to comfort her. After a short while, she moved away from me.

"Buzz, if you can, try to find her and see that she is ok."

"I will, Ma. Do you and Pa need any money?"

Ma looked at me. She told me that Pa wasn't bringing any income in, and her salary was minimal. Now that Helen was gone, things would get tough.

I gave Ma $500 .00 and promised I would keep money coming in, just as Mike had always done. With that, I said goodbye and went out into the cold autumn air. I would search for Helen, no matter how long it took. And, If I ever got my hands on Johnny, he would be dead meat.

11

Inclusion

So, the years dragged on. The 1940's became the 1950's. and the 1950's morphed into the 1960's. I continued to live in the apartment Mike had provided for me at The Rose. It brought many memories to me, but it was the only stable part of my life that had brought happiness, so I continued to live there.

Steve never suspected that I was out to revenge Mike's death, because I played my hand well. I carried out his orders of killing and heisting, grafting and shaking down to the letter like an automaton, hardly showing any emotion, hardly feeling any emotion. But, always in the background of my mind was the desire to kill him. I would not only kill him, but also I would make clear to him why I was killing him.

The boss asked me a couple of times why I never talked much. I always replied that I didn't have much to say. However, I began to wonder if he suspected that I was not entirely committed to him as his other bozos were. Maybe it was time to finish him off.

I began to pay more attention to his schedule. When was he at The Rose, and when was he in his Staten Island home? Of course, he was always surrounded in both places by armed men. It was probably a better plan to kill him when he was on the road, protected by only one bodyguard and a driver. I began to check his schedule with Joey's help.

Joey had become my sidekick in all the dealings I carried out for the Don. He never said outright that he hated the Don and what he was feeling in carrying out the Don's orders, but I had a strong hunch that Joey was getting more and more unhappy with the life we both were leading. The gang was deep into narcotics handling and distribution and Joey and I were the main dealers for Steve and his organization. There was also political graft, money laundering, gambling, and police protection schemes. There were frequent feuds with other mobs, but none who could touch Steve. Colin T. never got over our heist of his shipment of heroin, so there were frequent skirmishes between his mobsters and us.

Always in my mind was my single-hearted desire to kill the boss. It would happen eventually when he least expected it. I bided my time for the right moment.

I continued to hunt for Helen and Johnny. Through my police informers, I was able to track them down to Las Vegas. They had been married in the Little Church of the West, and had settled in a small house close to the El Rancho Casino and Hotel, on what came to be known as the Las Vegas Strip. Both Johnny and Helen worked in the Casino: Johnny as a croupier, and Helen who served refreshments to the gamblers. At least, that's how both of them got started. Why did I feel that Johnny would begin pimping Helen out to the biggest spenders in the Casino? They were married less than a year before he spread the information to the Casino's high-class clientele that Helen was up for the highest bidder. Helen was in her 20's when she married Johnny and she was becoming a beautiful woman. The years only brought full-blown beauty to Helen. The small house she and Johnny had bought was now expanded and fitted as a full-time brothel with Helen as the madam. She had six girls working for her. Johnny, sleaze bag that he was, roamed Las Vegas looking for women to satisfy the gamblers.

I met with Helen several times during the decades, but never when Johnny was around. Helen begged me to leave him alone. She was still in love with him, even though by now, she knew he was using her. That knowledge killed her, maybe because it partly brought back memories of her being used by our swindling parents. Helen and I both felt a deep sense of loss—she because she still loved Johnny and could never have the marital bond she so wanted, and I because I had lost Mike, the only friend and father I had truly had.

But I knew that no matter what, I would never

leave her, and never stop protecting her. So, I left Johnny alone as she asked me to, but I think she knew that if he ever tried hurting her, he would feel the full weight of my vengeance.

12

Revenge

It was in 1965 that I finally experienced the reckoning that I had been nursing and planning for years. Steve had lived a charmed life as head of his mob and in cooperation with the gangsters and his friend, Paul D. to continue his crime businesses. But the US government was beginning to put the squeeze on him by investigating his dealings through the efforts of stool pigeons and other disenchanted gang members.

I knew I would have to act before Steve was sent to prison. One day, the boss asked me to take a ride with him to Snug Harbor on Staten Island as his bodyguard. Joey was to drive. Steve wanted to check out some of his contacts, as well as to set up a new heist of drugs.

Of course, both Joey and I agreed, Joey because it was an honor to drive the boss and I because it was the opportunity I had been waiting for.

On our way to the Harbor, I asked Joey to pull over by a deep patch of woods, explaining to the boss that I had to pee. Joey asked if I could hold it in until we came to the next gas station. I said no and Steve agreed because he had to make a stop himself.

So, we both entered a section that was tight with bushes, trees, and grass to do our business. Steve had gone about 20 feet away from me. When he finished, he turned to me and faced my Beretta M934 pointed at his heart.

"What's this, Buzz? Some kind of joke?"

The boss's face was as white as I had ever seen it.

"No joke. I said. I have waited for years to do to you what you did to Mike, and in spades! You are going to feel the pain Mike felt when you exploded his head, I said calmly but very deliberately."

Steve began to scream for Joey and attempted to run toward the car. I pommeled five shots into his back and one shot deliberately into his head. I felt immense satisfaction. A large weight was lifted from me that I had carried for years.

Joey entered the clearing and looked horror stricken at what I had done.

"Are you crazy, Buzz? How are we going to explain how Steve was killed?"

"We'll say that a bozo from Colin T's gang followed our car, and shot Steve. Then you and I shot the hood and dumped his body into Narrows Bay. We will bring the boss's body back for him to have a grand funeral in a closed coffin."

Joey frowned, After a few minutes, he looked me square in the eyes and told me that story would never work

"Why did you kill Steve?" Joey asked me.

"Because he killed Mike. I have waited for this opportunity to kill Steve for years, and I finally have managed to do it," I answered.

Joey told me in a very low voice that he could not be partner to my story of killing the boss. We looked at each other. Then Joey turned to go back to the car. I felt badly because I had become closer to Joey through the years, but I knew he would never back me up. I took my pistol out and shot Joey twice in his back. He fell to the ground and died.

Now I had two bodies to dispose of, but a perfect alibi for Steve's death. I would say that Joey planned to kill Steve so he took advantage of our needs to relieve ourselves, followed us into the woods, shot the boss, and tried to kill me when I tried to intervene, but, instead, I was able to shoot Joey before he could kill me.

I went through Joey's pockets to find the keys to the car. Leaving the bodies where they lay, I went to the car, and drove to the nearest gas station where I put in a call to Steve's oldest friend, Paul D. to tell him with a strained, horrified voice that Joey had shot Steve and I had shot him. I gave Paul the directions to where the bodies were and asked him to send men to bring the boss to his home, as well as to get rid of Joey's body.

Paul couldn't believe what he was hearing. After a long silence, he told me his men would be there shortly, to stay with the bodies, and make sure no one was around to detect their removal.

I hung up the phone and drove back to where the bodies lay. My next move was to plant Joey's gun in his hand, after I had fired it six times into the bushes and to secure my gun in its holster.

I looked at Joey for a brief moment. We had become friendly through the jobs we did together. We had always watched each other's back. I felt twinges of shame, regret, and sadness that I had found it necessary to kill him, but I needed to do what I did. After finally killing Steve, I could not let myself be killed by the gang. Now, I would be celebrated for defending Steve and killing his supposed killer, and I would have also accomplished my revenge.

Paul and his men came quickly and looked over the entire scene. He heard me retell the exact details of what happened and checked Joey's gun for the number of bullets left in its barrel. He went over to Steve's body, and tearfully, silently viewed its carnage. Blood was still trickling from the wound in the boss's head, and his back was ripped apart by the five bullets I had pounded into it.

Paul turned to me, and stared at me quizzically.

"I can't believe that Joey did this" he said.

"Steve never told me that he felt Joey had any grudge against him. This killing is a complete surprise to me. Buzz, did Joey ever tell you that he wanted to kill Steve?"

I stood there frozen, hoping that Paul would not mistake my fear of being caught to confusion about Joey being the killer.

"No, No," I stammered. Joey never let on to me that he had anything against Steve so bad that he wanted to kill him."

Paul shook his head, then turned and gave orders to his men to bury Joey's body in the woods after they had taken his gun and all identification from him. He told his men to wrap the boss's body in the blankets they had brought, and drive him to his home.

Then Paul turned back to me and thanked me for avenging Steve's death. He kissed me on both cheeks, put his arm around me and led me to his car while directing one of his men to drive the other car to Steve's home.

13

The New Leadership

Steve's funeral was attended by many represen-
tatives of the prominent gangs to show their
respect as well as to find out who would be the next
leader of Steve's gang. After the funeral reception,
the leaders met in the Private room in The Rose.

I was in that meeting, as the one who had killed
Joey for having killed the boss. The leaders of the
gangs came to me personally and congratulated me
for my loyalty. Perhaps they wondered if I would
be the next head honcho? That was impossible,
of course, since I was still considered an outsider,
not someone who worked in the upper echelons
of the gang.

However, all the gangs had big problems by
the time Steve was murdered. Many leaders were

already dead through gang wars, and prison in-carcerations that had depleted likely successors. Intermarriages had also played a part in weakening their systems. Besides those realities were those of ethnic, criminal groups who were involved in the same type of activities that our gangs were. There were Irish, Chinese, and the Russian groups who gave us stiff competition in robberies, killings, and the drug trade.

Over all these complications was the challenge presented by the United States government. The government cracked down hard on the drug trade and other nefarious activities of the gangs, Protection from Law enforcement could not be bought so cheaply, if at all, as in former gang deal-ings. Some of the gang leaders had families whose adult children wanted nothing to do with the gangs in which their fathers were heavily involved.

All these predicaments faced the men in the room. Each leader presented his personal troubles about the difficulty of continuing business as usual. What had carried them through or their fathers through the Depression up to the present era was no longer viable now. It was a hard fact to face. Yet, it must be faced and decisions must be made to ensure their personal survival or to concede their diminishment.

So, with heavy hearts, each leader presented the toned-down activities his men would follow. No one could risk a takeover by the Law, or combat with the new groups that were forming. They would go underground, as it were, until that time when they either could rally in a united front, or quietly die out as a force to be reckoned with.

I looked around at the men in the room. They sat silently taking in what each leader had proposed. They knew their activities would not be business as usual. In fact, most of the leaders were old men by this time, and tired of having to be one step ahead of the Law. They calculated how many members each gang had, and the results proved disheartening. Maybe two of the gangs could survive as they were. The rest would need to fold. It was an historic moment because the realization of their past dealings could never be replicated with the power they once possessed, and now did not have.

Jack S., the present temporary leader of Steve's gang, rose to his feet, and in a serious, almost mournful voice, thanked the leaders present in the meeting. He asked them to make a decision with their men what they would do for the future and to report back to him so that they would not get in each other's way. For those who would disassemble their gangs and cease their activities, he wished a quiet ending.

After handshakes, hugs, and kisses on both cheeks, the leaders left the room. I turned around and faced Paul who was looking intently at me.

"Buzz," he asked. "What are you going to do now? Will you stay with Jack?"

Thoughtfully, I answered that I hadn't had time to consider what I would do next. I felt that I was at a crossroads. I had been in Steve's gang since I was 19 years old. Before that, Mike had taken me in when I was 13. Now I was close to 50.

Paul asked me if I wanted to join his men. He only had about five men, and he wanted me to be his right-hand man, since I showed loyalty to Steve by killing Joey Paul's group would take on smaller jobs and work undercover. I knew that Steve's gang was breaking up for lack of leadership, and attrition. Paul's invitation seemed like the right way to go, so I said yes. Paul was happy at my response and thanked me for accepting his invitation. I felt glad that I had found a place to work.

14

Advancement

As Paul's right-hand man, I was privy to all negotiations and dealings that occurred. Paul was a smooth operator. Up front, he was personable and liked by his men, as well by those he swindled. Underneath the façade, Paul was ruthless. He never let anyone's personal feelings, least of all his own, interfere with business at hand. I realized this fact very early in the game when Paul shot and killed his cousin Denny for not handing over a large sum of cash Denny had kept it for his family. Denny's sons were both in college and his wife could not afford to pay their tuition.

Paul greeted Denny very warmly, as usual one day, and when Denny gave him the money from a heist, Paul took it, counted it, and asked Denny where the rest of it was? Denny said that this was the amount he was given, looking straight at Pau's face.

"C'mon, Denny. That's crap. I know how much that heist was worth. What you gave me just now is bupkus."

"I swear to you, Paul. That's all I got. Why don't you believe me?" Denny was beginning to sweat, and tears were coming down his face.

Paul looked intently at Denny and said he was sorry Denny was lying to him. Paul wanted to know what Denny was going to do with the money he withheld? Denny answered that he needed that money to put his kids through college, and Paul wasn't paying him enough to support his family. By this time, Denny was already on his knees, bent over, and sobbing uncontrollably.

Paul put his hand on Denny's head to steady him, and told Denny that he was sorry that Denny didn't tell Paul sooner about his financial troubles and, instead, resorted to lying. Then Paul took out his Smith & Wesson 686 handgun and shot Denny twice in his head. Denny collapsed on the floor in a bloody heap.

Paul told me to take Denny's body to an exclusive

funeral parlor that the mob used and to fix up Denny's body for viewing. He told me to go to Denny's wife and to tell her Denny had been killed in the heist. He gave me the money Denny had given him to give to Denny's wife, and to tell her that he, Paul, would personally pay for her sons' tuition through to their graduation from college. He also instructed me to give Denny's wife a lump sum of one million dollars for her expenses. Paul would also pay for Denny's elaborate funeral.

Such was Paul's character. He could be generous to a fault, but no one had better double cross him. Not even family ties got in the way of that premise.

I did what Paul asked, but I got the very strong feeling that Denny's widow was not buying the fact that Denny had been killed during the heist. She knew Denny better, especially the fact that he was very concerned with paying for his sons' college tuition. She knew Denny did not want his boys to grow up as hoodlums, or to follow in his footsteps. She must have surmised that he had been keeping money back from every job he did to help his family, and that Paul finally realized what was going on. So, even though it galled her to do so, she accepted Paul's money gifts because she had to. She even forced herself to accept his condolences gracefully after the funeral when he approached her. Such was the double standard that gang members and their families lived by and continued mostly through fear.

I watched my own back as far as Paul was concerned, knowing that his charming personality hid a bloodthirsty killer. The jobs he sent me to do, I did to the letter. Paul often expressed satisfaction with my work, so I drifted easily into the role I played as his right-hand man. Even if there were legal problems associated with the jobs we did, Paul always found a way of straightening them out. His finger was always on what Law enforcement was actively engaged in, so that he could be one step ahead of it while protecting his interests.

Life was good during those years. I got rich, and I was always able to provide for my parents. Both Ma and Pa died within a year of each other during the 1970's. Pa never recovered from his beating and complete isolation, and he was a basket case by the time of his death. Ma stood by him, nursing him with the help of 24-hour aides that I provided. It was no surprise to me that Ma died within a year of Pa's death. They had been joined at the hip for close to 50 years, and she almost didn't know what to do with herself after he died.

I scarcely saw Helen during those years. Her business as a madam enlarged to such an extent that it covered several states, and she constantly traveled to maintain it. Helen hardened during that period. Johnny became a nonentity to her, a person she readily dismissed from any obligation as his wife. When Helen was consigned by Johnny to the highest bidder in Las Vegas, in spite of the heartache it caused her, she slowly became aware how worthless Johnny was as a husband and as a man. She began to exclude him from any contact with her or her business. She finally told him to get out of their house and never to come back. Johnny didn't put up a fight. He knew Helen had only to call me and he would be terminated. Also, he had begun relationships with hookers who eventually gave him syphilis. By the time he died, he was a nut job who didn't know his right from his left.

There were never any romantic interests in my own life. I had never learned to love anyone, except

Mike, from my earliest years. Steve and Paul weren't father figures to me. They were my bosses who taught me to kill and steal, basically. I was now pushing 60 and had never had a serious relationship with a woman. Some women had shown an interest in me, but I never let them get close to me. Deep down, I wanted to be loved for myself, but I was always afraid that either I would be taken advantage of, or that I would lose a person whom I loved just as I had lost Mike. And, I couldn't talk about my lack of love to anyone. Trust and communication are the bases for any relationship, and my lifestyle precluded both. So, I drifted along with the years, hardly feeling, much less having any emotional ties to anyone.

15

A Sendoff

Paul got older and more suspicious as the years went on. Twice he faced jail time, and twice was able to get out of it with the help of clever lawyers and fearful judges. That made him suspect everyone, including me. I put up with him because he was a dangerous man when crossed, and because I knew, ultimately, that one day in the near future he would be caught and locked up for good. I began to hope for that day because I was very tired of assuaging him constantly during the outbursts. He couldn't enjoy what his life of crime had given him in money and possessions, and he couldn't sleep at night because he was afraid that someone would get into his room and kill him. He was always armed and guarded by at least one gangster, mostly me since I was his right-hand man.

I was sick of him, to tell you the truth. His paranoia took a drain on me as well as on the rest of the gang. He had become a crazy old man who distrusted every one and often carried on like an idiot until I slipped him a 600mg Quaalude pill that put him in La La land for a period of time and gave the rest of us quiet until the pill wore off and he became more agitated than ever. Either one of two things was inevitable: either the Law would finally get him and lock him up, or his mind would totally destroy him. His dependence on drugs was rapidly leading him to his ruin. It was only a matter of time, but waiting for either occurrence to happen was excruciating.

One day, I went into his room to bring him breakfast, and he sat up in bed with that inane stare of his. Focusing his attention on me, he blurted out:

"You killed Steve, didn't you? Joey didn't have any reason to kill Steve. What was your reason, you double crossing traitor! And now, you want to kill me, don't you? There's poison in that food, isn't there? Get away from me! Get away from me!"

Paul kept yelling like a banshee. He got out of bed, lunged at me, threw the tray to one side out of my hands, and tried to grab my throat with almost superhuman force. I quickly jerked his hands off my throat and gave him a mighty shove backwards into his bed. His head hit the bedboard and he was momentarily stunned. Two of the guys came into the bedroom when they heard Paul's cries. They saw him staggered on the bed, and figured he was going through his ritual of suspicion. I told them I would take care of the boss and not to worry, so they left the room.

I turned to Paul and all the years that I had to deal with his craziness came to the fore. In that moment as I looked at his old, shrunken body and concentrated on his wild eyes, I knew I had to put an end to his life, for my sake as well as for the men in our gang. Before he could come to any realization of what I was going to do, I took the extra pillow that was on the chair by his bed and forcefully covered his face with it, using every ounce of my strength to bear down on the pillow.

Paul squirmed at first and tried to push away the pillow from his face, but I had the momentum, and he was too weak to subdue it. Slowly, slowly, he stopped struggling until there was no motion, no resistance coming from him.

"Crazy old fool", I said as I lifted the pillow and stared at his face. His eyes were open, and there was a look of horror on his white shrunken face. I would tell the men that he had a massive heart attack and was gone in three minutes. The look of horror could pass as the great pain experienced during the heart attack.

I called the men in so that they could pay their respects, even though I knew they hated Paul as much as I did. I told them that I would take care of a private burial for him, which, basically, meant that I would bury him quickly and quietly in a place known only to me. Since there were still some gangs operating, I would quietly communicate Pau's death to them.

To this day, no one knows where Paul is buried. No one will ever find his burial place. That is because I took his decrepit body during one night to the Fresh Kills land fill on Staten Island and tossed his body into the murky marsh before tons of garbage filled it in. To my mind, a garbage dump was the most appropriate burial place for Paul.

But, after his burial, I began to reflect on what he had blurted out about my killing Steve. Did he suspect that I had killed Steve and decided to keep me close until he could take his revenge on me as I had taken my revenge on Steve? Did he confide that fact to anyone else in the gang? There were only four of us left in Paul's gang. I began to scrutinize the other three guys for signs that one of them night carry out my demise.

All of us were now in our 60's. Two guys, Manny and Bud, had medical issues, and announced after Paul's death that they were "retiring" from active duty in the gang. I let them go and wished them well. Sal was left. Sal was a quiet individual. I don't think he ever got over the fact that Paul had made me his right-hand man instead of him. He had been with Paul for over five years when I appeared on the scene, and Paul abruptly made me the underboss. Was he nurturing a grudge against me, one so strong that he wanted me dead?

I decided to be wary of Sal. I asked him one day what he intended to do now that there were only two of us? He looked quizzically at me for a moment and replied that he was looking at several options, without telling me what his options were. Then he asked me the same question. What was I going to do now that having a gang with only two members was irrelevant? He looked intently at me when he asked his question, and, at that moment, a chilling fear went through my entire body. I sensed a deadly design in that question, and I resolved never to put myself in any situation where Sal could kill me. I was sure that he was going to try. I just had to be vigilant.

16

It's Over

All the King's horses and all the King's men,
Couldn't put Humpy Dumpty together again.

It is hard to describe the toll constant vigilance against Sal's predatory aim had on me. For 24/7, I needed to watch him and be aware that he was watching me. I had never been afraid of anyone or anything. Now I became suspicious of any unnecessary noise or movement. Night brought the most fear in me. I scarcely slept the entire night. Every shadow on the wall heightened my paranoia, every sound reverberated with twice its intended meaning. I scarcely ate because the food might have contained poison. True. I was not living close to where Sal had an apartment. The Rose was now an exclusive restaurant, whose gambling business was now turned into an attractive casino. The prostitution rooms were now expanded, select suites. I had moved out of The Rose about five years ago to where Paul had a private cottage. He had given it to me in a burst of generosity, so like him when he was coherent. But now, Sal knew where I lived and that fact added to my terror.

The days went by Usually, I stayed inside the cottage, my gun always by my side. On a cold winter morning, however, I decided to take a walk and to clear my head. I found myself walking by the schoolyard where the kids were having recess. Looking at that schoolyard brought back memories. Yes. I had been there years ago. However, the kids of the 70's didn't play Humpty Dumpty anymore. I doubt if they ever knew such a game existed. The words of the rhyme came back to me. Humpty Dumpty fell and no one could put him together again. Was that what was happening to me? Looking at the kids brought back memories of my parents, Helen, and Mike. I thought of my dealings with Steve, Joey, and Paul. I thought of myself and realized that I was still a Zero, a hollow man, an automaton, for what did I have to show for my life that was positive?

I was tired—not only physically tired, but also tired of life. I had not contributed anything worthwhile to society. On the contrary, I had murdered, plundered, and deceived people in the world that had been given to me by my parents. I was useless And then, I thought of Sal. Where was he today? I began to feel very frightened.

I continued looking at the kids playing at recess. It brought a strange kind of calm to me. Only when I noticed a teacher watching me from the schoolyard then I began to move away.

I walked and walked with no apparent destination until I was exhausted. Then I turned back to go to my cottage. I unlocked the door and went in to the living room. Sal was sitting on the sofa, his gun resting beside him.

We looked at each other, but I was quicker on the draw than he was. I shot him three times in his head and chest. Then I went to my bedroom where I had the picture of my parents, Helen and me on the dresser. I looked long and hard at that picture, and all the worthlessness of my life of crime over-whelmed me. I sat down at my desk and thought about what I needed to do. Killing myself was not an option. Should I give myself up to jail time for the rest of my life? Could I leave New York and start a new life?

17

What Now?

I decided to call Helen and to tell her what I was feeling. One thing was for certain: I could not stay long in the cottage with Sal's decaying body. Sooner or later, some of his friends would start looking for him, and his murder would provoke questions that ultimately would lead to me.

Helen answered the phone and I asked her to listen to what I had to say until I was finished without interjecting her response. I told her everything—all the murders, the thefts, the con jobs, the drug heists, —all of it since I was 19 years old. I told her of my great loss of Mike, and I reminded her of not being loved and guided by our parents, of my deep loss of having no family to love, support, and guide me. By the time I was finished, and for the first time in my life, I was crying uncontrollably.

Helen was silent. When I had quieted down, she asked me what I intended to do. I told her I didn't really know what I should do. That's why I called her. After more moments of silence, Helen began to tell me of the events in her life since her marriage to Johnny—of her life as a prostitute, then as a madam of a prostitution ring. She told me of her sense of degradation, of her feelings of worthlessness, of her desires for a family of her own that would never materialize. And, as always, the conversation turned to our family and the bitterness of never being loved by our parents.

After listening to each other we fell silent. Perhaps for the first time in our lives we realized that we had to move on. Our parents were dead, but we still had each other as we had always had. We were our family and would be no matter what came next for us. It was a freeing moment, a moment that brought us to what I had once read: "A moment's insight is worth a lifetime of experience."

After that beautiful moment, reality intervened.

What now? We both had to make decisions, and it was clear that we needed to make them together. Helen was in Nevada, but she could arrange her affairs in a few days and fly to meet me wherever I decided to go. What was clear was the fact that we wanted to be together for the rest of our lives. We would be the family that we never had. There would be no looking back. There was only a future to mold, a second chance to unfold.

I told Helen that I would call her back once I ironed out the details of where we would meet, and I hung up the phone. I felt happy, and uplifted. I didn't want to look back on my squalid life, but after a few minutes, and after looking at Sal's body bleeding out on the floor, all the weight of my crimes began to overwhelm me. Could I justifiably leave my past behind and begin again in a brighter future? A decision had to be made and quickly.

Should I give myself up to the police or join Helen to lead our lives peacefully at last. Perhaps we both could give back to society what we had never received. We both had enough money to live comfortably, but maybe that money could also be used to help those who needed it. We could help children especially who were not loved in whatever capacity that presented itself.

I thought of Mike and wondered if that is what he would do if he had ever gotten to Florida, and taken me with him. How different my life would have been. I started packing my clothes and gathering the essentials I needed for the trip. I went to my safe and took out the money and the papers I needed. Still, the questions haunted me. Could I just step out of my life of crime without making restitution? Was it fair to Helen to let her begin a new life without me? To leave her a second time when we were so close to starting a new life together? And, if we did leave together, where could we go where our identities and our dealings would be shrouded in obscurity?

I was becoming more and more confused, yet, I knew that I had to leave the cottage quickly. I turned to the front door and opened it. Snow was falling and the wind was cold. I shivered slightly, closed the door, and stepped out into the snow. My life was before me, but what form should it take?

On the way to my car in the driveway, I saw a little sparrow who had fallen from a bush and lay in the accumulating snow. I took him gently into my gloved hands and wiped the snow from his feathers. He opened his eyes and came to himself. He tried to flutter his wings, so I opened my palms, and after a moment, he flew away to the bush from where he had fallen. There, in safety, he looked at me and I looked back at him. Then I continued on my path.

The End

Photo by Edward Sudol.

www.ingramcontent.com/pod-product-compliance
Ingram Content Group UK Ltd.
Pitfield, Milton Keynes, MK11 3LW, UK
UKHW020950270125
454275UK00013B/430

9 798822 976351